I0673560

MEGHNAD SAHA

MEGHNAD SAHA

Scientist with a Social Mission

Dilip M. Salwi

Revised Edition

RUPA

Published by
Rupa Publications India Pvt. Ltd. 2015
7/16, Ansari Road, Daryaganj
New Delhi 110002

Sales centres:
Allahabad   Bengaluru   Chennai
Hyderabad   Jaipur   Kathmandu
Kolkata   Mumbai

Edition copyright © Rupa Publications India Pvt. Ltd. 2002, 2015

Text copyright © Dilip M. Salwi 2002, 2015

Photographs courtesy: Saha Institute of Nuclear Physics, Kolkata

All rights reserved.
No part of this publication may be reproduced, transmitted,
or stored in a retrieval system, in any form or by any means, electronic,
mechanical, photocopying, recording or otherwise, without the prior
permission of the publisher.

The views and opinions expressed in this book are the author's own and
the facts are as reported by him which have been verified to the extent
possible, and the publishers are not in any way liable for the same.

ISBN: 978-81-291-3666-4

First impression 2015

10 9 8 7 6 5 4 3 2 1

The moral right of the author has been asserted.

Typeset by Ninestars Information Technologies Ltd, Chennai

Printed at Repro Knowledgecast Limited, Thane

This book is sold subject to the condition that it shall not, by way
of trade or otherwise, be lent, resold, hired out, or otherwise
circulated, without the publisher's prior consent, in any form
of binding or cover other than that in which it is published.

To
a friend and well-wisher,
Dr Partha Sarathi Datta,
for his commitment to
scientific research and people

CONTENTS

Chapter One: Reaching Out for Stars   9

Chapter Two: The Born Revolutionary   15

Chapter Three: The Self-made Researcher   22

Chapter Four: Exit from the Ivory Tower   35

Chapter Five: Science to Serve People   44

Chapter Six: The 'Uncut Diamond'   58

Sayings of Meghnad Saha   62

Chronology   63

Bibliography   66

Acknowledgement   68

REACHING OUT FOR STARS

Two very young physics teachers of Calcutta University's Science College, Meghnad Saha and Satyendra Nath Bose, were very keen to take up scientific research. Both had done their master's degree in applied mathematics—or what is now known as 'mathematical physics'—and secured second and first positions respectively. Both of them were familiar with the revolutionary developments then taking place in physics in Europe—Max Planck's Quantum Theory, Niels Bohr's Atomic Theory, Albert Einstein's Theory of Relativity, etc. They were eager to know about those developments, teach them, and even try their hands at doing research in them!

Unfortunately at that time, there was nobody available in Kolkata to inform the young men—let alone teach them or guide them—about those developments in modern physics. Even the latest books on the subject were not available in their college libraries. After considerable search, one P. J. Bruhl, a German national, who taught physics in the neighbouring Sibpur Engineering College, was found to have a personal collection of the latest books on modern physics. But they were all in German! Fortunately, young Saha—who was popular among his friends as 'Eigenschaften' ('Invincible' in English) for his knowledge of German—had earlier learnt German, since in those days, it was considered to be the passport

to science. He, therefore, began to borrow modern physics books from Bruhl's library and started reading them. His friend Bose also began to learn German and read those books.

It did not take long for the two young men to become conversant with the latest developments in modern physics. In 1919, they even jointly translated Albert Einstein's Theory of Relativity into English—the first in the world to do so—so that they could teach the same to their students! Astrophysics, the physical and chemical aspects of stars, including the sun, and thermodynamics, the science of energy and its conversion into various forms, particularly fascinated young Saha.

Saha read the popular science books on astronomy and astrophysics by Agnes Clarke and came to know the cutting edge of research in these subjects. He learnt that, though sunlight and even thousands of star lights had been photographed and analysed, astronomers knew that these gave information about the chemical compositions of the sun and stars but they did not know how. Besides, there were several features—that were incomprehensible. Subsequent thorough study of the concerned research papers, published in the previous 25 years of a reputed journal of astronomy, brought young Saha face to face with the latest ideas and data on the subject. One particular paper drew his attention as it made an attempt to solve some puzzling features of star lights but somehow failed miserably.

Saha was wondering as to why the aforementioned paper failed to solve those puzzling features. At that time, he was teaching thermodynamics and spectroscopy, the study of sunlight and starlight, to his students. It was then that he hit upon the real reasons behind those unsolved

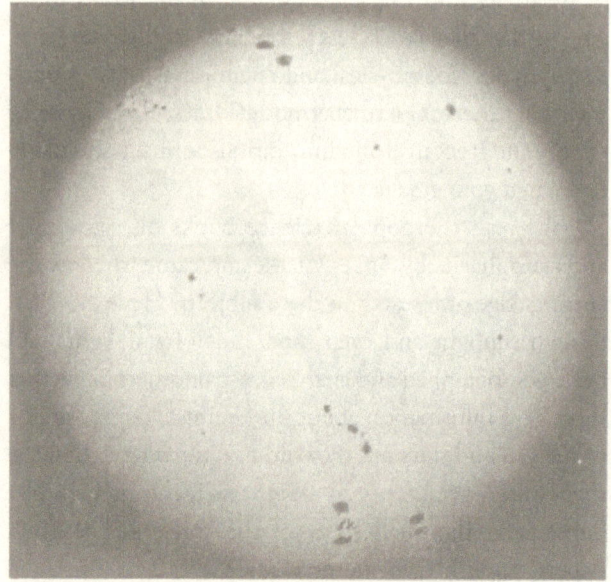

The sun - our 'special' star. Black spots on its surface are 'sunspots'

puzzles. Actually, he applied the latest ideas of modern physics to those astrophysical puzzles. To his utter amazement, he could solve the puzzles to a great extent by inventing a novel mathematical formula, which is now known as 'Saha's Ionization formula', named after him.

The formula helps to make possible the assessment of the chemical compositions of the sun and stars, their internal temperatures, pressures, etc., by observing the

Felicitation of Saha after his election to the Indian Parliament in 1952

light emitted by these heavenly bodies. At one stroke, the sun and stars no more remained mysterious objects. His work generated so much enthusiasm in the UK and USA that a spate of research papers followed. It was even hailed as one of the major milestones in astrophysics! In fact, it led to the birth of modern astrophysics. Saha's work was of considerable imagination based on the theories of physics and chemistry and tools of mathematics. Without any guidance and facilities, Saha went on to make a dent in the world of science. It showed what a person can achieve if he or she is committed to making a wonderful contribution.

Moreover, it was a commendable achievement for a person who was the first in his family to learn science and who came from a rural background. And he did not stop at being only an ivory tower scientist keen to win accolades of fellow scientists; but he took—an active interest in the social aspects of science and did his best to ensure that science was properly used for the welfare of his countrymen in Independent India. He not only initiated the creation of several scientific institutions in the country but also went on to become a Member of the Indian Parliament to serve people through science. He was a true son-of-the-soil scientist.

CHAPTER TWO

THE BORN REVOLUTIONARY

Saha was born on October 6, 1893, in a village of East Bengal (now in Bangladesh). This village, Seoratali, was about 40 kilometres from Dacca, where floods, mud, and slush were a common occurrence. As he was born on a rainy and stormy night, he was originally named 'Megha Nath', as 'Megha' means 'cloud' and 'Nath' was after family traditions. But young Saha renamed himself as 'Meghnad'—a famous character in a poem written by a renowned Bengali poet. Besides, Meghnad is also the uncompromising fighter-son of Ravana! And so Saha remained—an uncompromising fighter throughout his life, in science as well as social work and politics.

Saha's father was a petty grocery shop owner, who was somehow able to make ends meet and feed his big family of eight children. Being illiterate, he had no inclination to

Saha's parents: Bhubaneswari Devi and Jagannath

educate his fifth child, Meghnad. Moreover, his eldest son had not done well in studies. Thus, he felt that education was a waste of time. He was keen to train young Saha in running the shop and tending domestic animals. But from childhood Saha showed interest in learning. He would cry if a pencil or a book was not made available to him. Often, his father would beat him for disturbing his sleep, as young Saha was in the habit of reading the books loudly!

But Saha continued to do well in studies while he helped his father in running the shop and tending the cows. The teachers of the local school could not tolerate

The Simulia Shyamaprasad Middle English School, where Saha had his schooling

the fact that the talent of a bright boy was not being utilised properly. They persuaded Saha's father to send him to the neighbouring English medium school that was about ten kilometres away. Fortunately for Saha, the local doctor of that village, Anantha Kumar Das, offered him both lodging and boarding, free of cost, provided he performed some household duties.

As a child, Saha was fond of reading the heroic deeds of Rajput and Maratha warriors. He imbibed their spirit of a fighter both during war and peace. He also read the Bible and various Hindu religious scriptures, However, he developed an aversion to religious rituals from the day a local village priest did not allow him to sit on the dais during Saraswati Puja because of his caste. Even in

Presidency College, Kolkata

his youth he bore the wrath of temple priests and even classmates.

After, standing first throughout school, Saha joined the Government Collegiate School, Dacca, in 1905, on a free studentship. Those were the days when the British Government had decided to partition Bengal into two, East and West. Though administrative reasons were offered for the division, it caused considerable uproar all over Bengal. Demonstrations, meetings, boycotts, bonfires of British clothes and goods, etc., were held every other day to lodge a protest against the partition.

So, when the British Governor of Bengal, Sir Bampfylde Fuller, visited the Collegiate School, several students boycotted his visit in protest. A revolutionary at heart, young Saha, then hardly 12, could not resist joining the boycott. It led to his expulsion from the school. His free studentship was also cancelled. His brilliance in studies, however, helped him to gain admission to Kishori Lal Jubilee School, a private school, with a free studentship.

In 1909, he passed the Collegiate Entrance Examination with the first position in entire East Bengal and joined the Intermediate Dacca College for Intermediate studies. He also took private lessons in German language as in those days it was the language of science. In other words, young Saha was preparing himself to become a scientist from that early age of sixteen.

Two years later, Saha joined the Presidency College, Kolkata, to do his B.Sc. in applied mathematics. S. N. Bose, who also made a mark in the world of science, was his classmate. The eminent statistician P. C. Mahalanobis, who initiated the National Sample Survey and set up the Indian Statistical Institute later, was his senior by a year. The great physicist and inventor J. C. Bose and the great chemist, social worker, and industrialist P. C. Ray were

Saha along with his college teachers and classmates. In the centre is P. C. Ray; Saha is standing in the backrow (extreme left)

his teachers. In fact, in the evenings, he would often accompany his friends to meet P. C. Ray and discuss various issues about science and country. Once, he also joined Ray's team to bring relief to flood-affected victims in Bengal.

In those days, Saha had also become friends with several revolutionaries who were fighting for India's freedom. For instance, Pulin Das and 'Bagha Jatin' Jatindranath Mukherjee, who had once single—handedly fought and killed a tiger with a dagger in the jungles of Sundarbans, were his friends. The fiery Subhash Chandra Bose, who raised the Indian National Army later, was his junior by a year. Though Saha sympathised with their cause, he never actively took part in their activities because he had bigger responsibilities to shoulder at home. His elder brother was financing his studies. He himself intended to finance the studies of his younger brother, and besides, he was committed to science. However his revolutionary spirit could not stand injustice at any stage in his daily life. When some higher caste students in the Eden Hindu hostel did not allow him to share the dining table, he and his likeminded friends lodged a protest and joined a private hostel.

After college education, the brilliant Saha, like C. V. Raman, would have also joined the Indian Financial Service had he not boycotted the school and not been suspected of having links with the revolutionaries. He was denied permission to take the IFS examination by the British Government authorities. After M.Sc., he continued to live—in Kolkata, earning a living through private tuitions. He would pedal his bicycle to different parts of Kolkata to take private tuition classes.

CHAPTER THREE

THE SELF-MADE RESEARCHER

Finally, in 1916, Saha as well as S. N. Bose secured lectureship in physics in Calcutta University's Science College, all because of the efforts of Asutosh Mukherjee 'the Tiger of Bengal'. He was then the Vice Chancellor of Calcutta University and recognised the brilliance of these two young men. Initially, their appointment was made in the Department of Mathematics but they were subsequently shifted to the Department of Physics as they could not get on well with another mathematician, Dr Ganesh Prasad.

Thus began the brilliant careers of these two young, enthusiastic men who were passionately interested in modern physics. They were not only interested in learning the latest developments in physics but also wanted to impart their knowledge to students and conduct research in it.

Despite the absence of a modern library, no guidance in teaching or research, and no peers to discuss modern physics with, both made a mark in their chosen field. While S. N. Bose went on to make valuable contributions to quantum physics, Saha created a milestone in astrophysics. In 1917, he wrote his first paper, which was immediately published in the British *Philosophical Magazine*. Thereafter, Saha wrote a series of papers. One original yet long paper was accepted by the American *Astrophysical Journal* but could not be published as Saha was not able to pay its cost of publication in dollars. It was subsequently published by Calcutta University. That paper contained the seminal idea of the 'Theory

of Selective Pressure', which was later wrongly credited to an American astrophysicist. Nevertheless, his research output was original enough to secure for him the Doctorate of Science (D.Sc.) of Calcutta University in 1918.

It was however his classic essay On the Harvard Classification of Stellar Spectra', written under the pen

Saha as a young man in the 1920s

name of 'Heliophilus' as per the

entry rules of participation in the competition for Calcutta University's Griffith Memorial Prize, that brought accolades to him, both at home and abroad. It was not only accepted for publication abroad but it also fetched him the Prize as well as both Premchand Roychand Studentship and the Guru Prasanna Ghosh Fellowship. Besides, it also secured him the hand of a homely and

Radharani, the wife of Saha

beautiful Radharani Roy, Impressed by the two major honours rarely bestowed on a single scholar, Radharani Roy's well-to-do father gave her in marriage to Saha who was then trying to gain a foothold in the world of science.

With the fellowship money, Saha sailed for England in 1919. He had a keen desire to meet fellow scientists, exchange scientific ideas, visit laboratories, and conduct experiments to verify his ideas. During the sea voyage, somebody suggested that he should meet the eminent British astrophysicist Professor Albert Fowler of Imperial College of Science and Technology, London. When he met Prof. Fowler, the latter thought he was keen to do D.Sc. under his guidance, as any Indian would have loved to do. But when Saha did not show any such inclination Prof. Fowler lost interest in him.

Prof. Fowler's interest in Saha was awakened some time later when one of Saha's papers was published in the *Philosophical Magazine*. Realising that the young Indian had something original to contribute to astrophysics, he encouraged Saha to pursue his ideas further. He offered Saha constructive criticism, gave him the latest data, and even allowed him to use his personal library of books on spectroscopy and astrophysics. In the next four months, Saha went through the entire literature on the subject.

Those were the days when astrophysics was in the primitive stage of development. It was the great 18th century British physicist Isaac Newton who showed that when sunlight is passed through a triangular glass prism, it splits into an array of seven colours—Violet,

Sunlight passed through a glass prism is split into seven colours, called spectrum

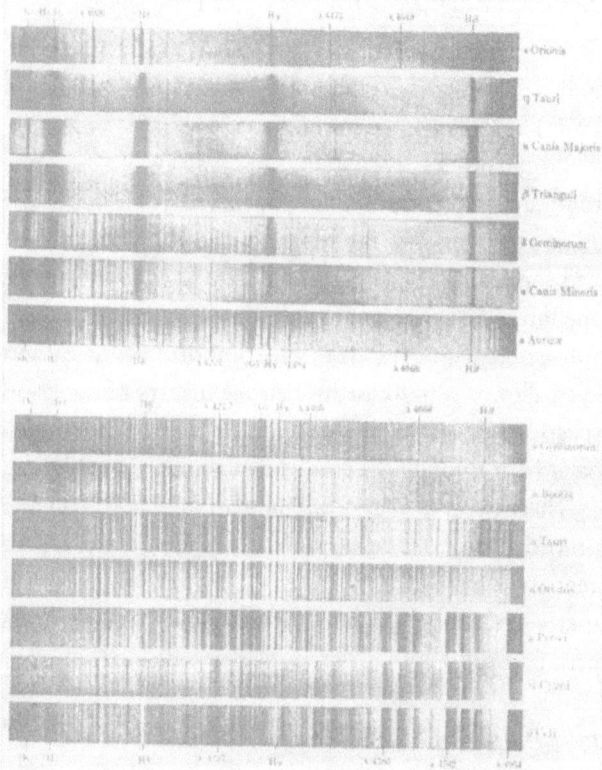

Spectral lines of a variety of stars

Indigo, Blue, Green, Yellow, Orange and Red—called 'spectrum'. The phenomenon is similar to the formation of a rainbow when sunlight gets split by droplets of water hanging in the air. But it was the 19th century German spectacle—maker Joseph Fraunhofer who closely studied the spectrum and discovered fine dark lines in it, now called 'Fraunhofer lines'.

Fraunhofer was closely followed by his two countrymen, Robert Bunsen and Gustav Kirchhoff. They also studied the spectrum produced by a candle or burner flame and found that it also contains some dark as well as bright lines. They found that those lines in the spectrum, called 'spectral lines', were characteristic of the chemical elements present in the flame. In other words, they had discovered a tool, called 'spectral analysis', to ascertain the elements present in a substance by burning it in a flame and studying its spectral lines. Subsequently, spectral lines were also found beyond the visible range of colours, that is, in ultraviolet, infrared and X-rays. Although these studies were conducted in laboratories and helped chemists in analysing the composition of substances, they raised a hope among astronomers that spectral analysis of sunlight and star lights would also provide information on their chemical compositions and internal conditions.

In the meantime, photography was invented. Now it became possible for astronomers to take photographs of the spectrum of the sun and stars, called 'spectrographs', and maintain their records for future study. The 19th century American astronomer Henry Draper, working at the Mount Wilson Observatory of Harvard University, U.S.A., made a huge catalogue of the records of spectra of the sun and stars and also classified them. The classified catalogue is known as the 'Harvard Classification of Stellar Spectra', which was the subject of research of Saha's Griffith Prize—winning essay'.

In the early part of the 20th century, astronomers knew what the spectra of the sun and stars looked like but not what they meant or what information they provided about heavenly bodies. Moreover, some spectral lines were thick, some thin, some diffuse, some very bright, and so on. According to the then accepted ideas about the interiors of the sun and stars, some lines were present where they should not have been and some were absent where they should have been present. In short, spectral lines were then a puzzle to the best brains in astrophysics. All kinds of ideas, including fantastic forces, were forwarded to explain the mechanism behind the formation of the spectral lines.

Agnes Clarke's popular science books, available in the library of the Science College, had introduced young Saha to these puzzles and fantastic ideas. In fact, they had provoked him into thinking about their origin and mechanism. He had begun to read further the latest researches on solar and stellar spectra. It was the research paper of the little known astrophysicist J. Eggert, a student of the eminent German physicist and Nobel Laureate Walther Nernst, published in a 1919 issue of the German journal *Physikalische Zeitschrift*, which brought the real problems into focus before Saha. As in those days, he was teaching thermodynamics and spectroscopy to his students at Science College, he applied their basic principles to these problems. And then a revolutionary yet simple idea flashed into his mind and made him immortal in the annals of astrophysics.

At that stage, the eminent Danish physicist Niels Bohr had forwarded the idea that an atom—the smallest bit characteristic of its chemical element—has a central, heavy nucleus with electrons orbiting it at various levels, and the eminent German physicist Max Planck claimed that energy is emitted or absorbed in small packets, called 'quanta'. Saha, then 27, applied these newly emerging ideas of modern physics to the interiors of the sun and stars in order to explain the puzzling spectral lines. He theorized that due to the extraordinarily high temperatures existing inside the sun and stars, the outermost electrons of atoms gain this energy and leave them. In other words, atoms get ionised and become positively charged ions.

This phenomenon of 'ionisation' occurs most frequently in the outermost layers of the sun and stars where pressure is comparatively low. But pressures inside the sun and stars are extremely high, which compress the ionised atoms together, bringing the free electrons closer to the nucleii. The latter, therefore, traps the electrons back, reversing the process of ionisation set off by the prevailing extremely high temperatures. In other words, the behaviour of the ionised atoms—and there are several scores of different atoms of chemical elements, namely, hydrogen, helium, caesium, rubidium, etc., present in the sun and stars—is different in different regions. This variety of behaviour of the ionised atoms—or simply 'ions'—in different regions of the sun and stars is therefore. displayed in the wide array of puzzling spectral lines.

Using mathematical tools, Saha developed a formula, what is now known as the 'Saha's Ionisation formula'. He included in his formula a well known physical chemistry concept, called 'Ionization potential'—the minimum energy required to knock an electron off an atom and convert it into an ion; it varies from one atom of a chemical element to another. This simple concept when introduced explained the presence of the puzzling spectral lines. It gave birth to Saha's 'Theory of Thermal Ionisation' and an atomic interpretation of the spectral lines. It transformed spectroscopy into a precise, quantitative method of investigating the physical and chemical conditions inside the sun and stars.

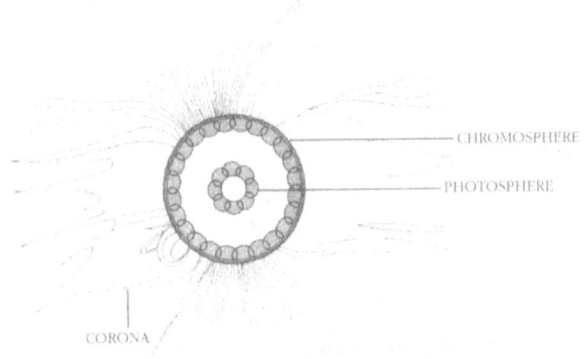

Different layers of the sun's atmosphere: 'photosphere' is the yellowish round seen with naked eyes; 'chromosphere' is the reddish layer above it (seen during a solar eclipse); and 'corona' which is clearly seen during a solar eclipse

To put it simply, Saha's formula gave new insights into the interior of the sun and stars, their chemical compositions, densities of various elements, and gravitational forces on their surfaces. Subsequently, when he applied his formula to the sun, he showed how the difference in pressure between the interior of the sun—, its outer atmosphere, the chromosphere, was responsible for the different spectral lines they exhibit. This also led to the creation of his 'Theory of Selective Pressure', another major contribution to astrophysics. Saha's theory gave some verifiable predictions. For instance, it predicted the presence of spectral lines of some elements which would only be found in the regions of lower temperatures in the sun. Those elements were eventually found in the sunspots—the dark, comparatively cooler regions on the surface of the sun.

On Prof. Fowler's suggestion, Saha withdrew his Griffith Memorial Prize-winning paper 'On Harvard Classification of Stellar Spectra' from publication in the *Philosophical Magazine*, revised it in the light of latest findings and submitted it to the prestigious. Royal Society of London under the new title 'On a Physical Theory of Stellar Spectra'. The Society invited Saha to give a lecture and immediately published his paper in its prestigious proceedings. It created a big stir in the astrophysical circles. His line of thought was immediately picked up by other astrophysicists especially in the UK and the USA.

Saha firmly believed in the great mathematician W. R. Hamilton's dictum: 'Theory and experimental investigations are the two eyes of physics, and research works flourish best when workers can see with both eyes.' He was, therefore, very keen to set up experiments to verify his ideas about ionisation very high temperatures and pressures in a well equipped laboratory in England. But he could not obtain the necessary facilities even in the prestigious Cavendish Laboratory and so went to Walther Nernst's laboratory in Berlin, Germany.

In Germany, Saha stayed for about a year and conducted his pioneering experiments, which led to the creation

Saha with eminent physicists in Europe

of a novel subject, called 'Laboratory Astrophysics'. It has today become the cornerstone of astrophysics because, after all, any science whose foundation is not in experimentation is futile. In Germany, he rubbed shoulders with several distinguished physicists, such as Albert Einstein, Max Planck, Max von Laue and Arnold Sommerfeld. He gave lectures at various science forums, and also participated in debates and discussions on science and scientific research. Back in England, he also met the eminent astrophysicist Arthur S. Eddington and his assistant Edward A. Milne of Oxford University, who went on to extend Saha's theory and formula with another astrophysicist R. H. Fowler.

The real work on Saha's formula, however, started at the Mount Wilson Observatory, USA, where the spectrographic records on stars were available in plenty. It was Henry Norris Russell of Princeton University, who immediately recognised the 'golden key' in Saha's formula to unravel the puzzling spectra of stars. He initiated a combined attack of physicists, chemists, and astronomers on the formula to unravel the mysteries of stars.

Slowly and steadily, the confusion prevailing around the spectra of the sun and stars began to clear up. In short, Saha's paper became a guiding light for all astrophysicists. Even some eminent astrophysicists of the time, namely, Arthur S. Eddington and Norman Lockyer, considered it to be one of the ten major milestones in astrophysics. Saha's pioneering work thus gave birth to modern astrophysics.

CHAPTER FOUR

EXIT FROM THE IVORY TOWER

The news of Saha's wonderful scientific achievements reached India. In 1921, the Vice Chancellor of Calcutta University, Asutosh Mukherjee, offered him the Khaira Chair of Physics, which had meanwhile fallen vacant in the Science College. Saha immediately returned home and joined the college. But in due course he realised that he could not see eye to eye with C. V. Raman, who was then a Palit Professor of Physics in the college. Besides, the university was undergoing a financial crisis. He did not even get his salary in time not to speak of securing the services of a laboratory assistant or buying any equipment for the laboratory he intended to set up. Two years later, he began to look for a post in another university. Of the several prestigious

Saha with his colleagues of the Department of Physics, Allahabad University

ones, such as Benaras Hindu University and Aligarh Muslim University, which offered him professorships, he opted for Allahabad University where some of his former classmates were teachers.

The Physics Department of Allahabad University was well equipped for teaching physics and conducting practicals but that was all. It was not at all equipped for conducting research in modern physics. Hence, initially, Saha faced considerable problems in securing funds, and facilities, even students, to conduct research on problems that interested him. The administrators of the university were unable to appreciate his research work. For instance, when Saha found the University library containing outdated books he ordered the latest ones, but the administrators told him to first read all the books in the library before ordering new ones! On another occasion, Saha placed an order for four pieces of the electrical equipment, 'Post Box', for the laboratory. Being unaware of the scientific equipment, the administrators asked him why he needed four postboxes to send his mail! Even Saha's reputation as a scientist was questioned as most of the people failed to understand and appreciate what he had achieved in astrophysics—the subject often mistaken for astrology!'

Gradually, Saha overcame these hurdles by sheer determination, commitment and persistence. He received a real boost as a scientist and a teacher when the prestigious Royal Society of London elected him as its Fellow in 1926. His original research papers were found referred to, or quoted, as many as 225 times by other astrophysicists in one year. In fact, he would have been elected two years earlier had suspicions about his links with Indian revolutionaries not come in the way of his election to the Society. Not only the local Government of the United Provinces (now Uttar Pradesh) under the British Raj woke up to his existence and offered him some funds on a yearly basis but also the Royal Society gave him some grant to set up his laboratory. His very name also began to attract talented students to Allahabad University.

Although adept at theoretical work involving mathematics and requiring paper and pencil only, Saha was very particular about the need for science practicals and experiments. He used to urge his students to take experiments as the final answer to any scientific query since he knew that Indians avoided working with their own hands and looked down upon it. To emphasise that ancient Indians were also very particular about experiments, he often used to quote the following passage taken from a 9th century Sanskrit text *Rasendra Chintamani* that said.

'I have heard from the lips of savants; I have seen many formulae well established in scriptures; but I am not recording any which I have not done myself. I am only recording those fearlessly which I have carried out before my elders with my own hand. They are alone to be regarded as real teachers who can show by experiments what they teach. They are the deserving pupils, who having learnt from their teachers can actually perform them and improve upon them. The rest are merely stage actors.'

And Saha did not merely preach, as is evident from his previous attempts to verify his theory of thermal ionisation experimentally, both in England and in

Saha with eminent astronomers and astrophysicists in Cambridge, U.S.A.

Germany. Even during his stay at Allahabad University, he set up a well equipped laboratory on spectroscopy and another on upper atmospheric study. Both these subjects are related to his favourite subject of ions and ionisation.

At that stage, Saha also wrote a research paper on the need for setting up a 'stratospheric solar observatory' at an altitude of 40 kilometers above the earth using balloons to study the spectrum of the sun above the filtering and disturbing effects of the atmosphere. What he had expected to see in the ultraviolet spectrum of the sun came true eighteen years later when Americans used the German *V2* rockets to photograph the sun. In recent times, several observatories, including the Hubble Space Telescope, have been set up in space from time to time to conduct various studies of the sun and stars. But when he had first floated this idea way back in 1937, he was called an 'idle dreamer'.

As a teacher, Saha always prepared his lectures thoroughly and systematically. He would often write down what he spoke on the blackboard in his clear, bold handwriting. He would also make use of lantern slides and was fond of demonstrating experiments during his lectures. His house at Allahabad, called 'Science Villa', was always open to students. He also offered every kind of help to a deserving student.

Saha guided several research students in spectroscopy and ionospheric studies. Ionosphere is an electrically charged layer of ions surrounding the earth, which reflects radio waves and makes communication on the earth possible through them. Among his students who went on to make a mark in science in India were D.S. Kothari, P. K. Kichlu, R. C. Majumdar, N. K. Sur. When he found his students suffering due to lack of good Indian textbooks, he also wrote a few, jointly with his students. *A Treatise on Heat*, written in collaboration with his student B. N. Srivastava, is considered, even today, a classic textbook on the subject for science undergraduates and postgraduates.

Besides physics, Saha loved ancient history. He was very fond of visiting places of historical and archaeological importance. In fact, he would ensure that he visited the important sites and monuments whenever he travelled in

India or abroad—in the Middle East, Europe or USA. His interest in ancient history and astronomy stimulated his interest in the history of the modern calendar vis-a-vis those followed in India and other countries. Observing the irregularities in various calendars, he used his knowledge of astronomy to rectify and reform the present Indian Saka calendar containing timings of *tithis, nakshatras, yugas*, etc. Much later, after India gained independence, he also chaired the national committee on calendar forms. The committee went into the nitty-gritties of various calendars and gave suggestions and recommendations to the then newly formed Government of India in form of a report in 1955.

Having seen the vital role that various science academies and societies, such as, the Royal Society, the French Academy, the Prussian Academy and the Russian Academy, played in building a strong scientific community and in directing researches in newly emerging fields after the Renaissance in European countries, Saha realised the need for such an academy in India. But the idea took firm roots only during the Indian Science Congress meeting held in Allahabad in 1930. Two years later, he founded the United Provinces Academy of Sciences at Allahabad, with the assistance of the local British Government.

Subsequently renamed the National Academy of Sciences, Saha organised a symposium on 'Power supply'

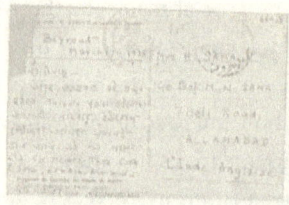

A picture postcard sent by Saha to his wife from abroad

in 1934 under its auspices. The purpose of the symposium was to bring all experts of related fields together and collect their suggestions and recommendations for generation and distribution of electric power for the development of the United Provinces. The inspiration to organise this symposium was drawn from a speech of Jawaharlal Nehru, a promising young Congress politician then, when he had urged scientists and technologists to give tangible proposals for the economic development of the country. This was Saha's first concrete step towards using science and technology in the service of his countrymen.

Of course, Saha already had the inclination to do so because soon after his return from Europe in 1922, he had given the Presidential address On Means of National Upliftment' to the Bangiya Yubak Sammelan organised by Subhash Chandra Bose. In this address, he had said that science held a key to all kinds of progress and his countrymen should adopt it for improving their lives. Later, in 1935, he also set up an academy of all

India character called 'National Institute of Science' in Kolkata. It was later renamed as 'Indian National Science Academy' and its headquarters were shifted to New Delhi so that it could influence the people in power.

It was however the speech of Dr Kailash Nath Katju, the then Minister of Industries of the first Congress Government in the United Provinces, which turned out to be an eye-opener for Saha and expedited his exit from the 'ivory tower' of a research scientist. Sitting on the dais adjacent to the Minister during the inauguration of a match making factory, Saha was aghast to hear the Minister's comments about heavy industry that reflected his total ignorance! Suddenly, it dawned upon him that if the reins of the country were left in the hands of such politicians, who were abysmally ignorant about science and technology, they would lead her to ruins.

Saha, therefore, decided to give up his 'ivory tower' of scientific research and take active part in bringing the benefits of science and technology to the common man. It was a rare realisation for a scientist who always wants to make a major contribution to scientific thought, win accolades and honours from his fellow scientists, and do not care two hoots whether his work benefits the common man or not. Saha was then thirty seven— young, energetic, and enthusiastic to take up the new task of applying science to the service of the Indian masses.

CHAPTER FIVE

SCIENCE TO SERVE PEOPLE

In 1938, when Saha was offered the Khaira Professorship of Physics at Science College of Calcutta University, he came back to Kolkata with a strong desire to start teaching and research in nuclear physics. During his last visit to Europe and the United States, he not only attended a major conference on nuclear physics at Copenhagen, Denmark, but also visited the high energy laboratory of E.O. Lawrence, the inventor of the 'atom-smashing machine' Cyclotron, at Berkeley, USA. He had become convinced that nuclear energy had assumed the centre stage of science in the West because it could generate tremendous energy for the production of electric power.

In fact, to spread awareness about nuclear energy amongst Indian scientists, Saha gave lectures and talks, as and when he could, on its latest developments that

The Cyclotron at the Saha Institute of Nuclear Physics, Kolkata

he saw in the western countries. He was actually waiting for an opportunity to introduce nuclear physics in teaching curriculum and research. He even sent one of his students, B. D. Nag Choudhary, who later became the Defence Adviser to the Government of India, to work under the guidance of Lawrence and learn the assembly and working of cyclotron for various nuclear studies. In 1940, he was able to introduce nuclear physics as a special subject in the post-graduate classes. It should be borne in mind that he made these attempts much before the first nuclear bombs were exploded over the Japanese cities of Hiroshima and Nagasaki in 1945, when the world actually realised the awesome power of nuclear energy.

Saha (extreme right) in front of the magnet of the Cyclotron, Institute of Nuclear Physics, Kolkata

Later, a cyclotron was also set up in, what is today known as, the 'Saha Institute of Nuclear Physics' in Kolkata, with the assistance of Lawrence and funding of the Tata Trust. It is said that Nehru helped him procure the funds from the Tatas through his political connections. The parts of the cyclotron however look considerable time to reach India due to the Second World War. Once, even the US ship carrying some parts was sunk by Japanese bombers. Despite war, red tape, and scarce funds, Saha finally managed to set up the Institute of Nuclear Physics on Acharya Prafulla Chandra Street in Kolkata in 1950. The institute was inaugurated by the

Nobel Laureate Irene Joliot Curie, the eminent physicist and daughter of madame Curie.

Despite his pioneering efforts at introducing nuclear physics to Indian students and scientists, Saha was sidelined after independence. Although he introduced the first courses in nuclear physics in the country, he was ignored while setting up the nuclear science base. Saha believed that to build a strong nuclear science base, India requires highly skilled technical manpower and a strong industrial base, which the country did not have at the time of Independence. Thus, he was highly critical of the policies of Nehru, the then Prime Minister of India, when he favoured another nuclear physicist Homi j. Bhabha in setting up a nuclear science base on a war footing. Today, history has proved him wrong as he misjudged the abilities of Bhabha and Indian nuclear scientists.

Meanwhile in 1943, the Damodar river went into spate, its flood waters surrounded even Kolkata and cut it off from the, rest of India. During his childhood, Saha had a first—hand experience of the havoc caused by floods, how they affected daily life, disrupted families, caused shortages of food and fuel and led to greater poverty. As a student of P. C. Ray, a college teacher and popularly known as 'Doctor of floods', Saha had participated in providing relief to the flood—affected people. So he felt unhappy that even after some decades, floods continued to haunt

A recent issue of Science and Culture

his countrymen while the. Government had no permanent solution. to offer. He realised that only a systematic, scientific study of the Damodar river system and its neighbourhood would bring floods under control and save his countrymen from the resulting misery. Moreover, he thought of harnessing the flood waters for the benefit of his countrymen.

Saha took upon himself the task of studying the flood problem of the Damodar river in totality because it also caused soil erosion and siltation. In addition to the study of the topography of the region, the annual rainfall at various spots, etc., he set up a small hydraulic laboratory in the college to simulate the actual conditions and understand the problem. He also conducted a first-hand survey of the region and even studied the various flood control measures of river systems in the western world. On the basis of his painstaking research, he wrote a series of articles in his own, newly launched monthly *Science and Culture*. The articles dealt with how the flood waters of the Damodar river valley could be controlled and harnessed for irrigation, navigation, and electric power generation, taking the model of the Tennesse river whose flood waters had been controlled and harnessed in the USA. He also proposed the creation of a hydraulic laboratory in Bengal for studying the problem in depth on a regular basis. To sensitise his colleagues, friends, and students to the menace of floods, he also set up a model of the Damodar river system in the corridor of Science College!

Due to his incisive and indepth articles, which advocated the Bengal Government to take some concrete steps to prevent floods, Saha was selected as a part of the Government committee to look into the matter. As suggested by him, the Damodar Valley Corporation was set up in 1948, on the model of the Tennesse Valley Authority in the USA, and the Bengal River Research institute was also established at Haringhata, near Kolkata, to conduct studies on flood control.

Saha's scheme of controlling floods in Damodar river valley and harnessing its water to generate electric power

It is a wonderful example of how science can be harnessed to the needs of people provided scientists leave their ivory towers and spare some time to deal with the day-to-day problems that afflict the masses.

Till his death, Saha continued to write articles, editorials and essays in *Science and Culture*, the monthly journal of the Indian Science News Association that he had founded in Kolkata in 1934. A journal modelled on the prestigious British science journal *Nature*, it publishes the latest researches as well as news and views on science and technology issues. In this journal, Saha regularly wrote on various aspects of science, how science could be utilised in the development of the country, and commented on the science policies and programmes of the newly set up Indian Government. His comments, observations, and criticisms were based on his personal studies, researches, and convictions. He always called a spade a spade and never compromised on any issue. Politicians, bureaucrats, and persons in authority, whose vested interests were hurt, therefore, disliked him.

Meanwhile, Saha had also become the President of the Indian Association for the Cultivation of Science. He was not satisfied with its old accommodation at Bow Bazar Street and was keen to reorganise its functions on a larger scale. The Government of West Bengal came to his aid when it gave ten acres of land for the Association,

On the Scientific Goodwill Mission to the U. K. Indian scientists in the picture are Nazir Ahmad, J. C. Ghosh, M. N. Saha, S. S. Bhatnagar and J. N. Mukherjee in the front row (L to R)

adjacent to the Jadavpur University campus, and also granted funds for the construction of its building and research facilities. Subsequently, in 1953, Saha was made its Director.

When India gained Independence in 1947, Nehru became the first Prime Minister. A person educated as well as interested in science, he was, like Saha, keen to use science for the service of his countrymen. In fact, he had placed Saha in several national committees and boards concerning science and technology for the reconstruction of India, such as, the National Planning Commission, Department of Scientific and Industrial Research, even before the country gained Independence.

Saha hits headlines in an American newspaper

On his recommendation, Saha also became a delegate of the Indian Scientific Mission that visited the UK, and USA and the erstwhile USSR to study the various scientific organisations there.

But in due course, Saha's outspoken nature and open criticism of the Indian Government's science policies and plans through the pages of *Science and Culture*, cast him into the shadow. Saha felt that Nehru was in a hurry to establish a scientific and technological base in the country without taking into account the prevailing culture and infrastructure. Moreover, he felt Nehru had a soft corner for Gandhian ideals, which he was firmly against. Nehru

On the opening day of Central Glass and Ceramic Research Institute, Kolkata, in 1950. From left to right: B.C. Roy, Justice C.C. Biswas, S. S. Bhatnagar, Jawaharlal Nehru, M. N. Saha and Atmaram

therefore did not favour him as much as he favoured Bhabha, S. S. Bhatnagar, and P. C. Mahalanobis in developing the scientific and technological foundation in the newly Independent India.

Since the formation of the USSR (now Russia) in 1917 and her subsequent reconstruction and technological advancement through application of science for the welfare of the masses—and not for a profit motive or efficiency in war—she had impressed Saha considerably. Although not a leftist or associated with any political party, he saw in the USSR his ideal of a welfare state and was keen that India should emulate her.

Saha was also against the Swadeshi movement based on Gandhian philosophy, which was gaining popularity amongst the Congress leadership and the masses before the Independence of India. He felt that this movement would do nothing else but bring back *Vedas, khadi, charkha* and bullock carts to the country. He was keen on modernising India and so believed that the country should go full steam at heavy industrialisation following the example of the USSR. Like Subhash Chandra Bose, he believed the country should follow the Soviet style of planned development.

Unfortunately, Saha has been proved wrong on both counts in recent times: the collapse of the USSR and her economy and the popularity that Gandhian philosophy and ideals, even in the matters of technology, have gained all over the world. The popular concepts of 'Small is beautiful' and 'Technology with a human face' have roots in Gandhian philosophy.

Even before Independence, Saha had visualised the problems of poverty, unemployment, and diseases that a backward country like India would face if she gained Independence. But when he asked Subhash Chandra Bose, the then Congress President, about what the newly elected Congress intended doing about them if

Saha addressing a gathering at Maidan, Kolkata, in 1952

the freedom was won, he replied that nobody had time to think about them! On Bose's suggestion, he then addressed an assembly of Congress workers on these issues. His historic speech, 'Rethinking Our Future', was subsequently published in the form of a pamphlet in 1953 and freely distributed among politicians and social workers. In fact, earlier, in 1938, this speech was instrumental in setting up the National Planning Commission, which even today draws plans for the scientific and technological development of the country.

After Independence, Saha realised that if he had to make any meaningful contribution to the reconstruction and development of the country, he had to enter the

Indian Parliament. He agreed to stand for the first Parliamentary elections of Independent India on the suggestion of the Congress leader, Sharat Chandra Bose, the brother of Subhash Chandra Bose. However, a senior Congressman flatly refused to give him a Congress ticket on the grounds that he held anti-Gandhian ideals. He, therefore, stood as an Independent candidate from the south-west Kolkata constituency and won by a big margin over his nearest Congress candidate and entered the Parliament in 1952.

Till his untimely death in 1956, Saha fought for various issues—from the re-settlement of East Bengali refugees to foreign involvement in the oil refinery at Bhavnagar—on the floor of the Lok Sabha and made his presence felt in all debates and discussions. Particularly, he challenged the licenses given to several foreign companies for exclusive entry to Indian markets. Although several Parliamentarians urged him to go back to his physics laboratory on the floor of the Parliament, he stood firm like a rock, and fought them. He also gave an address to the Parliamentarians on the 'Future of Atomic Energy in India' to acquaint them with this newly emerging subject, which would play a vital role in the country's development. At this time he was not keeping well due to high blood pressure. He died of a heart attack in New Delhi on February 16, 1956, while on his way to the

Planning Commission on Parliament Street. His death was a day of mourning for the entire country, especially Kolkata, where he was a popular figure. All festivities of Saraswati Puja came to a halt in the city. He was survived by his wife, three sons, and four daughters. His eldest son Ajit Kumar Saha, who became a nuclear physicist, went on to assume the Directorship of the Saha Institute of Nuclear Physics.

CHAPTER SIX

THE 'UNCUT DIAMOND'

Although Saha died as an internationally renowned scientist and a national figure, he remained an 'uncut diamond' till the end—a village boy, who wore simple clothes and lived an austere life. He never lost contact with his village Seoratali throughout his life and even built a girls' school there and named it after his mother, Bhubaneswari Debi, who had once sold her gold bangles to pay his examination fee.

He believed that man is the maker of his own destiny, and so led a life of discipline and commitment. He always woke up early, would go for long walks or jogging, perform exercises, and once in a while, would get himself massaged by an expert masseur. His students looked at him with both awe and affection. At times he appeared harsh and rough because he did not tolerate irresponsibility but he would always guide a student till he had not learnt the ropes. But once he realised that the student was on the right track, he would give him a free hand to do research. He also ensured that his students get good job openings in science. Not interested in sports or films, he always urged his students to play games and not to waste their time on watching others play.

Saha built two schools of research, one at Allahabad and the other at Kolkata. He applied new concepts and techniques of one scientific field to another, enriching the latter in many ways. His fields of research were diverse— from astrophysics, spectroscopy, ionosphere, cosmic rays, elementary particles, carbon-dating to ancient history and archaeology. Although he built and managed several scientific institutions and academies, his dream of setting up an Institute of Biophysics and a Radio Astronomy Centre failed despite the preliminary efforts he made in these newly emerging fields.

Saha had a vision of a strong scientific base in the country and made every effort to turn it into a reality. He believed that fundamental scientific research should continue in the universities and should feed trained manpower to scientific institutions and organisations in the country. Unfortunately, after the Independence of India, his words never counted. There appeared a mushroom growth of scientific institutions in the country under Government patronage at the cost of universities. Today, on one hand, the universities are suffering as no research continues there and, on the other hand, they are unable to provide trained manpower required for scientific institutions. The strong scientific base that Saha envisioned in the country could, therefore, not be built, leave alone the fact that not a single scientist working in India since her Independence has won the Nobel Prize.

Saha was a scholar par excellence and wrote on all aspects of national life, including the Constitution of India. He had a profound knowledge of economics, history, and social science. He wrote in both Bengali and English for newspapers and radio to acquaint a common man with the latest happenings in science. For instance, as far back as in 1919, he wrote a popular version of the newly propounded Einstein's Theory of Relativity when it was confirmed by a total solar eclipse; he wrote on the story of the atomic bomb when it was dropped on Hiroshima in 1948; and the industrial utilisation of atomic energy in India when in the same year he was offered—but had declined—the membership of the Atomic Energy Commission.

All major libraries in Kolkata and the Parliament library in New Delhi were his regular haunts. Before he spoke or wrote on a subject, he always did a thorough study of its background. Unlike most Indian scientists who always keep their knowledge to themselves, Saha always tried to share his scientific knowledge and was always at ease whether he was communicating with his fellow Parliamentarians or people on the street. Throughout his life, he kept the needs of a common Indian uppermost in his mind and was keen to apply science to fulfil his or her needs.

But Saha did not merely write like a scholar, or a writer, or a journalist, he even pushed himself into various committees and programmes to convert his ideas and suggestions, etc, into concrete action plans for implementation. He was indeed a scientist with a missionary zeal.

SAYINGS OF MEGHNAD SAHA

'Free thinking is good but right thinking is better.'

'Science and techniques are as important for
administration nowadays as law and order.'

'You have to be at your work.
Recognition is sure to come.'

'The keyword of the present civilisation is science.
In order to survive, we have to struggle
with nature and to win this battle we must
have science as a tool.'

'Science is a matter of many minds: there is no such
thing as super genius in science. A scientist who is very
good in one subject may be an absolute fool in another.'

LANDMARKS IN MEGHNAD SAHA'S LIFE

1893	Born on October 6 at Seoratali, near Dacca, in the erstwhile East Bengal (now in Bangladesh).
1909	Stood First in Joint Entrance. Examination in the erstwhile East Bengal.
1915	Stood Second in M.Sc. examination, Calcutta University.
1916	Joined Calcutta University's Science College as a Lecturer.
1917	Published his first research paper in the *Philosophical Magazine.*

1918	Received D.Sc. from the University of Calcutta on basis of his thesis on radiation pressure and electromagnetic theory. Also, published in collaboration with S. N. Bose the first English translation of Albert Einstein's Theory of Relativity.
1919–1920	Forwarded his famous 'Theory of Thermal Ionization' and proceeded to Europe on a fellowship.
1921	Returned to India to join Calcutta University's Science College as Khaira Professor of Physics.
1923	Joined the University of Allahabad as Professor and Head of the Physics Department.
1927	Elected a Fellow of the Royal Society, London, and went abroad to Europe and the USA.
1931	Founded the U.P. Academy of Sciences at Allahabad, which was later renamed as 'National Academy of Sciences'.
1934	Elected the General President of the Indian Science Congress Session held at Pune.

1935	Founded the National Institute of Science at Kolkata, which was later renamed 'Indian National Science Academy' and shifted to New Delhi. Also, established the Indian Science News Association at Kolkata and its monthly journal *Science and Culture*.
1950	Founded the (now Saha) Institute of Nuclear Physics at Kolkata.
1952	Elected a Member of the Parliament as an Independent candidate from northwest Kolkata constituency.
1953	Retired from Calcutta University and became the Director of the Indian Association for the Cultivation of Science, Kolkata.
1956	Died in New Delhi on February 16.

BIBLIOGRAPHY

Some eminent Indian Scientists,
Singh, Jagjit, Publications Division, 1966

Collected Works of Meghnad Saha,
Edited by Chatterjec, Santimay
Orient Longman, 1982

Maghnad Saha, Chatterjee, Santimay and Chatterjee,
Enakshi ,
National Book Trust, 1984

Meghnad Saha in Parliament,
Compiled & Edited: Chatterjee, Santimay and
Gupta, Jyotirmoy
The Asiatic Society, 1935

Special Issue on M. N. Saha,
Journal of Asiatic Society, Vol. XXXV (2)

Saha and His Formula, Venkataraman, G.,
University Press, 1995

Meghnad Saha, Karmohapatro, S.B.,
Publications Division. 1997

ACKNOWLEDGEMENTS

The author is thankful to Dr Kamales Bhaumik of Saha Institute of Nuclear Physics, Kolkata, for the photographs published in the book.

www.ingramcontent.com/pod-product-compliance
Lightning Source LLC
Chambersburg PA
CBHW020706260626
47157CB00008B/3159